# The Magic Wishbone

## By C.S. CROOK

Carolyn Sue Crook.  The Magic Wishbone

ISBN-13: 978-1503278837

ISBN-10: 1503278832

In this story, magic happens and dreams come true. A little girl makes a wish for the first time ever on Thanksgiving Day, with her mother using a magic wishbone. She refuses to say what she wished for and insists that the magic needs time to happen, although she doesn't understand exactly how magic works.

Two days later, new neighbors arrive at the ranchette next door and they own a pony with the marking of a wishbone on its forehead. The little girl, Hazel, is spellbound by the fact that the pony's name is Wishbone. She knows the pony is meant for her, because a pony was exactly what she wished for.

Another girl is jealous that Hazel may get the pony that she wished for and sets out to foil her dream, so that it does not come true.

Hazel and her friends also find three orphaned raccoons and raise them on a bottle and have to figure out a way to reintegrate them back into the wild.

This is a story of strong friendships and compassion for humans and animals alike.

Other books in this series of Johnny's Adventures are, 'Johnny's Reptile Adventure', 'The Skipper's Captain', 'Johnny's Heroic Adventure', and 'Finding a Home.'

# Contents

# Chapter 1

Hazel was in the kitchen helping her mother put away the leftovers from their families Thanksgiving dinner.

"Look at what I have!" her mother exclaimed, holding something up in her hand.

"Look at what? What is that? "Hazel asked, both puzzled and confused at the same time.

"It's a magic wishbone."

"What kind of magic?"

"Well, any kind of magic you want."

Hazel's curiosity got the best of her. She walked up closer to her mother and peered intently at the wishbone. "How-how does it work?" she stuttered. Hazel was so excited that she could hardly contain herself.

Her mother said, "I hold one end, and you hold the other end. We both close our eyes, make a wish, and pull the bone apart. But the wish only comes true for the person who gets the longest part of the bone when it breaks."

"Let me try?" Hazel eagerly reached for the bone.

Her mother chuckled and extended it to her. "Now take a firm hold, close your eyes and make a wish. When I count to three, we will pull, OK?"

"Okie dokie." Hazel smiled and closed her small fingers around one end of the bone. She squeezed her eyes shut real tight and made her wish.

Hazel's mother counted softly, "One, two, and three."

Hazel pulled until she heard a sharp snap.  Her eyes flew open, and she dangled her half of the bone between the tips of her fingers.  She surveyed its length and then looked eagerly at her mother's half of the bone.  Hazel jumped into the air and squealed with delight.

"I won! I won!" She chanted, as she bounced with joy around the kitchen.

Her mother laughed and asked, "What did you wish for?  It has to be something great!"

Hazel stopped bouncing and looked soberly at her mother.  "I can't tell you, or my wish will not come true."

The next morning Hazel's mother went to Hazel's bedroom to wake her for breakfast.

"Darling, wake up.  Breakfast is ready."

Hazel slowly opened her eyes and rubbed the sleep from them, lazily.  Suddenly, her eyes flew open, and she cried out, "Oh," and sprang out from beneath her covers.  She stood on her bed and peered intently out her window.

"What are you looking for?"  Her mother asked.

"I'm looking to see if my wish came true!" Hazel replied.  Then, a look of sadness washed over her face as her eyes searched the landscape taking in the old deserted ranch next door, with a for sale sign swaying in the gentle breeze.  "But I do not see it," she said weakly.

"What did you wish for, honey?  You know you can tell Mommy anything."

Hazel sank down to the bed and sadly shook her head no.  "I can't tell you or it will not come true."

"Well, come have something to eat," her mother coaxed.

All that morning as Hazel played, she kept looking out the windows, checking the yard.  After lunch, she took her cardboard

# The Magic Wishbone

sled and met up with her other friends at the mouth of the trail. She was eager to ask them what they all thought about magic wishbones, but she wanted to wait until Johnny joined them on the top of the hill. They reached the top of the hill and formed a line to take turns sliding down the slick, long golden grass to the bottom of the hill. Just as Hazel was poised and ready for her takeoff, she saw Johnny, with Trouble at his side; emerge from the grove of eucalyptus trees. She launched off from the top of the hill on her sled. Johnny stopped and watched her decent toward him and his constant companion. A wide smile spread across Johnny's lips. He loved watching her long, red ringlets bounce around behind her as she flew down the hill. She landed at the bottom and looked up at him with her large, emerald eyes. "Why did you stop just then? I was aiming for you," she said teasing him.

"Do you think I didn't know that? And besides, you would have mowed down my good dog."

Hazel smiled, stood up and reached out and petted Trouble. Just then, Bobby called out from the top of the hill, "Hey, if you two lovebirds are done, would you mind clearing the path?" Hazel and Johnny could hear the other children at the top of the hill giggling.

Hazel blushed and Johnny said, "Pay them no mind." Hazel picked up a corner of her sled and together she and Johnny headed toward the top of the hill.

Once they were at the top of the hill, Hazel asked, "Has anyone here ever heard about magic wishbones?"

Donna was the first one to speak up, "Sure everybody knows about magic wishbones."

Hazel replied, "Well, I didn't know about them until my mother told me about them last night."

"Did you make a wish?" Donna asked eagerly.

"That's just an old wives tale, "Fred said.

Hazel's face fell instantly.

3

Leslie said, "Don't pay any attention to what Fred said, Hazel. He thinks he knows everything."

Johnny spoke up and said, "I've heard about magic wishbones before, Hazel."

Fred rolled his eyes, and put his sled in position in preparation for a takeoff. "Well did you make a wish?" Donna pried.

"Yes I did, but it did not come true."

"Things like wishes can take a long time sometimes to come true," Johnny said. Hazel smiled brightly at Johnny and he could have sworn that his heart skipped a beat in his chest. "What did you wish for?"

"I can't tell anyone or my wish will not come true."

"Oh, you can tell us, we are your friends," Leslie said.

Lester, Leslie's twin brother said, "She is right. Everyone knows that you can never tell what you wish for, if you want it to come true."

Leslie spun around and glared at her brother and said, "When did you become the authority on wishes, Lester, hmmm?"

"You just don't want her wish to come true, Leslie," Donna said.

Leslie demanded to know, "Why on earth do you say that about me, Donna?"

"I say that about you because that is the way you are, Leslie." The other children nodded their heads in agreement with Donna. Leslie slammed her cardboard sled on the ground and pounced on top of it and took off down the hill.

Bobby had to scramble out of the way at the bottom of the hill to avoid a collision with Leslie's inbound sled. "Hey, Leslie, you know the rules. You are supposed to wait until I'm out of the way before you launch off."

Leslie hissed at him, "Maybe you're supposed to move faster."

Bobby shook his head in disgust and said, "I don't understand you." He picked up his sled and started back up the hill. Leslie trailed along behind him.

The children played on the hill the rest of the afternoon, with Trouble romping down the hill barking happily alongside Johnny, every time Johnny had a turn. Soon it was time that Johnny had to part company with his friends and Hazel watched as Johnny waved from the bottom of the hill and slipped into the woods with his ever faithful companion at his side. Hazel and her group of friends headed back down the trail and to their respective homes.

Darkness fell and still there was no magic. After her mother tucked her into bed and turned off the light, Hazel squeezed her eyes shut and to herself she repeated her wish.

The following morning stillness was broken by the crow of a rooster. Hazel groggily opened her eyes. She thought she had dreamt it, but then she heard the rooster crow again. They lived in the county, but they didn't have a rooster anywhere nearby.

Still half asleep she stood up on her bed and looked out her window. There on a fence post between her house and the property next door stood a beautiful, big red rooster.

He ruffled his feathers and puffed out his chest and greeted the morning sun very loudly again.

There was also a moving truck in the driveway of the house next door. Men in uniforms were busy carrying furniture into the house. Another huge truck was just coming around the bend, very slowly. Hazel had never seen a truck like that. It gingerly crept into the driveway. The truck had a van attached to it. The van had windows all along its sides and the windows had bars over them.

"I see you're already up," her mother spoke from the doorway of Hazel's bedroom.

Hazel turned to look at her mother and then turned her attention back toward the window. "Look Mommy!" Hazel pointed a small finger toward the window and the property beyond. "What kind of truck is that?"

Hazel's mother came over to her bed to peer out the window. "Oh look, we have new neighbors!" Hazel's mother exclaimed.

"What kind of truck is that?" Hazel asked again.

"Well honey, there are two trucks. One is a moving van and the other is a long distance horse van. Our new neighbors apparently have horses.

"It has horses in it? Hazel looked up at her mother with eyes that were dancing with excitement.

"Yes," her mother responded.

Just then a tall sender lady walked around to the side of the horse van and lowered the first bared window. A bay pony eagerly stuck his nose out of the window and tasted the fresh air. It whinnied so loudly that it startled the rooster and he fell from his perch on top of the fence post.

Hazel's mother chuckled at the comical sight. Then she felt Hazel clasp one of her arms tightly with her two small hands.

"Mommy," Hazel said, all most breathlessly. "There is my wish."

"What? What are you talking about?"

"My wish has come true!" Hazel exclaimed. "My wish has come true!" Hazel was so overcome with joy that she leaped from her bed and threw her arms around her mother's neck, nearly knocking her mother off balance.

The beautiful little bay pony had a white marking of a perfect large wishbone on his forehead.

"You wished for a pony?"

"Yes."

Hazel was on the floor tugging at her mother's arm. "Let's go get it, Mommy. Let's wake up Daddy, and go get it.

"Honey, the pony belongs to them."

"But Mommy, I wished for it."

Hazel's mother, Jenny, sank to her knees in front of Hazel and took her by both of her hands. "Hazel, not all wishes come true."

The joy on Hazel's face fell off. It just slid right down to the floor. It did not drip off like tears, but rather slid off in one sheet.

The sudden sadness that washed over Hazel's face was a hard sight for Jenny to witness.

# Chapter 2

"We need to introduce ourselves to our new neighbors, but we need to give them a chance to settle into their new home. They must be exhausted. It looks like they have come a great distance."

Hazel sullenly climbed back up on the bed and stood as if spellbound, peering out the window.

The lady next door continued to let the other barred windows down. Next to the bay pony, a buckskin pony with a blaze face stuck her head out and nipped at the nose of the bay. Next to the buckskin pony, a big sorrel horse, also with a blaze face, stuck his head out and looked around.

The big sorrel curled his upper lip up displaying some gigantic yellow teeth. The buckskin pony flattened her ears and nipped at him.

"OK, Dakota, everyone knows you're the boss, no one has forgotten," the tall lady said to the buckskin pony.

"Every one of you must be tired and grumpy. What do you say we check out your new home, shall we?" The lady walked to the back of the horse van and unbolted the back double-doors. She led the sorrel out first. "Take it easy, Sunny."

Sunny stepped gingerly out of the van. His head was held high and his ears were straight forward and alert. He snorted and pranced in circles around the tall lady. His tail was held high and flowed behind him.

Hazel held her breath as she watched. He was magnificent.

The sorrel horse was magnificent, but the brown pony was for her. She just knew it. She felt it in her heart. She had wished for it. She knew her mother was right that not all wishes come true, but magical wishes were different." She felt her heart lift with her new insight.

"Let's have some breakfast. And after we get dressed, maybe we can go over and introduce ourselves to them," Hazel's mother suggested. "But we can only stay just a few minutes. They have much to do."

Hazel jumped down from the bed, "Great idea Mommy!"

"Hazel, you scoot off to shower while I wake up your father and get breakfast on."

Hazel showered and dressed in record speed. She could smell the aroma of bacon floating down the hallway. She hoped there would be pancakes to go with it. She thought that would be so much better than eggs. She walked into the kitchen. Her father was up and just pouring his first cup of coffee. And to her delight, there were golden brown pancakes stacked tall on a platter in the center of the table. The pancakes were still steaming and butter was dripping down the sides.

"Yummy, Mommy," Hazel said, as she hugged her mother around the waist. Her mother planted a kiss on her forehead.

"I heard that we have new neighbors," her father said.

"Yes sir, and they have horses too. One big horse and two small ones," Hazel said, as she sat down and started piling her plate high with pancakes.

"Oh, and they have a really big chicken, Daddy."

"Rooster," her mother corrected her.

"Yah ah, a daddy chicken a real big one."

Her father sat down at the table. "Is that so?"

Hazel replied, "Yep, he woke me up bright and early."

C. S. Crook

"I guess he can get you up for school when it starts," her mother said, as she joined them at the table.

"Do the new neighbors have any children?" Hazel's father asked, between sips of his coffee.

"I didn't see any," Hazel replied.

"Well, that's curious," her father said.

"Why?" Hazel asked.

"Because you said that they have two small horses and one big one. Are the two small ones ponies or foals?"

"What is a foal?" Hazel asked.

"A baby horse," her father replied.

"Do you think the big one is a mommy horse?" Hazel asked, with her mouth full of pancakes.

"Young lady, what has happened to your manners?" her mother asked firmly.

Hazel sat her fork and knife down on the table. "Can we go over there now, Mommy?" Hazel's eyes were ablaze with excitement.

Her mother looked sternly across the table at her. "We may go over when we have all had a chance to enjoy our breakfast."

"Besides kiddo," her father chimed in, "they just got here. We've got some time to get over there to meet them."

Her parents chuckled. She didn't see the humor in it. She took up her fork and picked at her breakfast. She was already full, but decided it was best to be polite. If she got sent to her room for misbehaving, that would just be torture.

At last her mother asked, "Has everyone had enough, so that I may clear the table?"

"Yes!" Hazel exclaimed. "Let me help you, Mommy."

10

Jenny smiled and said, "My, the new neighbors could be a good thing."

"Yes, indeed," her father agreed.

"I think so too," Hazel said. Her eyes were sparkling like diamonds on a lake.

"Shall we?" her father asked.

Hazel squealed with delight and bolted for the front door.

"Where are your shoes?" her mother called out behind her.

Hazel slide to a stop on the wooden floor and blushed slightly. The three of them laughed.

As the family walked past the moving van, Hazel's father noticed the license plate on the back of the van. "Wow, it looks like they have come all the way from Oklahoma."

"I think they are going to enjoy the warmer winters that we have here," her mother replied.

Hazel's family walked up to the house, taking care to stay out of the way of the men in uniforms moving the furniture into the house.

"Oh honey, I don't think we are stopping by at a good time," Hazel's mother said to her.

Just then a pleasant looking older gentleman appeared from the doorway of the house. He extended his hand to Hazel's father and shot them all a warm and charming smile. "You must be the folks from next door?"

Hazel's father took his hand and the elderly gentleman shook it vigorously.

"Yes, we are the Richardson's. We just wanted to welcome you and your family to California. I am Ray and here is my wife Jenny and our little one is Hazel."

"The pleasure is mine. I am very pleased to meet you. My name is Jerry Adolph. My wife Mary is around the back with the horses. That's where you can usually find her," he chuckled.

"Can we go see her?" Hazel bounced up and down.

"Don't be rude, Hazel," her father said.

Jerry's smile widened, "Nah, she's not rude. She has been bitten by the horse bug. The same as with my Mary and I'm afraid there is no cure."

"Did a bug bite me?" Hazel asked, with alarm in her voice, and craned her head searching her body for any obvious bite marks.

All three adults laughed.

"No, honey, he means that you are horse crazy." Hazel furrowed her brows and looked up at her mother puzzled. Her mother reached out and ruffled Hazel's hair with her hand. "That means that you like horses. You are a silly goose."

"I love horses! I don't just like them, I love them! They are so very beautiful."

"Well, you folks go ahead and go on around back and I will join you shortly. We will be finishing up here in a bit. I just have to show them where to put the heavy furniture."

"Understood, we will let you get to it." Ray Richardson smiled and shook Jerry's hand again. "The pleasure is ours." With that the family turned and followed the gravel driveway around to the back of the house.

They saw Mary inside a horse stall. She was shaking sawdust out of big white plastic bags onto the floor of the stall. Sawdust was flying everywhere. She looked up and gave them a huge welcoming wave and a dazzling smile. "Howdy," she called out to them.

They returned her welcoming wave and Hazel dashed ahead. She ran up to the paddock fence and climbed up several rails and hung there by her arms. She studied Mary. She saw the worn cowboy boots, faded jeans and western shirt with the white, pearly buttons. Hazel liked the sky blue felt cowboy hat with the hat band made of peacock feathers. The beautiful hat was pushed back off Mary's forehead and sat atop a thick pile of shiny silver hair.

Mary looked at her and smiled. Mary's blue eyes twinkled when she spoke to Hazel's parents as they drew closer. "Shy, isn't she?"

"Sorry, we don't mean to be rude," Hazel's mother spoke softly.

"Oh heavens no, that's not what I meant. She's as cute as button."

"I'm horse crazy!" Hazel announced proudly.

Mary laughed and then stated, "Well, then you have certainly come to the right place. My name is Mary and I just happen to be a riding instructor."

I'm Hazel and here comes my Mommy and Daddy.

"Oh!" Mary's surprise and delight lit her face.

"I'm Jenny Richardson, and my husband is Ray."

"Well, I'm mighty pleased to meet the group of you. You folks live right here next door?"

"That would be us," Ray said.

Mary brushed some sawdust off her arms.

"What are you doing?" Hazel asked.

"Oh just trying to get the sawdust off me. It just gets everywhere. It especially gets inside my boots. Not to mention down my blouse too."

"Why are you putting it all over the ground?" Hazel asked.

"Oh, I was just putting bedding down for the horses," Mary replied. "I do it so they have a soft place to sleep at night."

"I always thought that horses sleep standing up," Ray said.

C. S. Crook

"True that they can sleep while standing up; sometimes they like to lie down as well, if they feel safe doing so."

"Wow, that's cool. I wish I could sleep standing up. How come they can?" Hazel asked.

"They evolved to sleep standing up so that they could flee their predators," said Mary.

Jenny extended her hand to Mary. "We just wanted to come over and welcome you to California. I think you'll love it here."

Mary took Jenny's hand and shook it and replied, "We will enjoy the winters for sure. It can really get cold in Oklahoma."

"Where are the horses? Hazel asked.

Mary motioned with her thumb toward the other side of the barn. "The herd is on the other side of the barn, having some lunch and settling into their new surroundings."

"Why are they having lunch?" Hazel asked. "We just finished breakfast."

"The day at a horse stable starts very early," Mary replied.

"That's why you have the rooster? It wakes you up? Hazel asked Mary.

"Yep, that he does. He wakes me up bright and early."

"What is his name?"

"His name is Sunrise."

Hazel smiled approvingly at Mary.

"Well kiddo, we can't overstay our welcome. The Adolf's have to get moved in today," Ray said.

Reluctantly, Hazel climbed down from the fence.

14

### The Magic Wishbone

Mary picked up her rake and leaned on it. She spoke warmly to Ray, "It certainly has been a pleasure to meet you and your lovely family. And please feel free to stop by anytime. We would love to have you."

Mary watched her new neighbors walk away. The adorable little girl turned and vigorously waved goodbye to Mary. Mary reached her arm above her head and swept the air high over her blue felt hat with the beautiful peacock feathers.

# Chapter 3

After lunch, Hazel met her friends at the trailhead.  She felt like she was almost bursting with the news about her wish coming true, but she wanted to wait to tell everyone all at the same time.  But mostly she wanted to tell Johnny.  She didn't want to spoil that by letting him hear it from the other children.  They could see that Johnny and Trouble were already on the top of the hill as they approached.  Johnny and Trouble sprinted toward them.

As Johnny drew near, Hazel flashed him the brightest smile.  Her whole face just lit up, making her look so pretty.  "Johnny, my wish came true!" She told him.

"Wow, it did?"

"Yes, it did!" The children stopped in their tracks and eagerly gathered around Hazel.  They all seemed to be talking at once, but they were all asking the same question.  They wanted to know what it was that Hazel had wished for when she made her wish.

"I wished for a pony."

"Wow, you got a pony?" Bobby asked.

"Well, not exactly, I don't have him yet.  I don't know quite how magic works, yet.  I wished upon a magic wishbone and two days later some new people moved into the little ranch next door to us. The magic is working, because the lady is a riding instructor and one of her ponies has the shape of a wishbone on his forehead."

Leslie said, "So your wish really didn't come true.  He is not your pony!"

Donna spoke up and said, "Leslie, surely even you can see a clear relationship here?"

"What relationship, Donna?  The pony does not belong to Hazel."

Johnny spoke up in defense of Hazel. "The magical relationship, Leslie, is that the pony has the shape of a wishbone on his forehead."

Hazel said, "Like I said, I have no idea how magic works, but something tells me that it is. I just have a feeling that it is working."

"Is the pony beautiful?" Donna asked.

"He is the prettiest pony I have ever seen," Hazel replied.

"I just love horses," Donna said.

Johnny said, "I'm sure your wish is coming true. Maybe it just needs some time to work itself out."

Hazel asked Johnny, "Do you like horses?"

Johnny shrugged and said, "Their alright, I guess, as long as they are not wild-eyed."

Hazel chuckled and asked, "What does wild-eyed mean, Johnny?"

He shrugged again and said, "I guess it means that you had best not get on one with wild-eyes."

Donna asked, "Is the pony wild-eyed, Hazel?"

"No, Donna, he has big round soft eyes, like a deer has. Come on let's go ride our sleds." When the children were done playing, they scattered in the direction of their respective homes.

Later that evening, Hazel's family sat around the dinner table. Hazel's mother had a suggestion. "I am going to make lasagna for dinner tomorrow night. I think I will make an extra tray for our new neighbors. They have so much to do with just moving in and all."

Her father said. "I think that would be a fine idea. It will give them a chance to take a load off."

"I have an idea! Why don't we invite them over for dinner?" Hazel asked.

"Moving is very hard work. We need to be respectful and think of all that they have to do. But we will have them over very soon," Jenny replied.

"Do you think Mary will let me ride one of her horses?" Hazel asked hopefully.

"She did say that she was a riding instructor," Jenny said. "The horses are her business, so perhaps you might be able to take some riding lessons from her. What do you think about it, Ray?"

Hazel jumped to her feet. Unable to contain her excitement she ran around to the other side of the table where her father was sitting and tugged at his arm. "Please Daddy, please?" she begged.

"Well from the looks of it, I have a feeling that if I said otherwise I would be cast from the house," he chuckled.

Hazel's mother smiled and gave him a nod of agreement.

"Does that mean, yes? Yes I can?" She was jumping up and down, as if she was on a trampoline. She was almost overcome with joy.

"Yes, that means yes!" Her father's smile reached his eyes.

Later, Hazel lay in bed looking up the ceiling, but was not seeing it. Her mind was racing ahead. She was thinking about the next day; like a movie being fast-forwarded on the TV screen while you were watching it. Then, her mother entered the room to tuck her in for the night.

Hazel propped herself up on one elbow, so that she was facing her mother. "Can we go over first thing in the morning, right after breakfast or maybe even before?" she asked hopefully.

Her mother came over and sat down on the side of her bed. "We will go over after I make the lasagna. That will not be until after lunch."

"But, Mom, that is such a long time to wait!"

"No buts, I want the lasagna to be freshly baked for them. You will live."

"Ahhh," Hazel sighed and sank down onto the bed.

Her mother pulled Hazel's covers up to Hazel's chin and tucked her into bed. You will survive," she said, and leaned over to kiss her forehead. "Goodnight."

"Goodnight, Mommy."

Her mother turned on her night light; switched off the overhead light and closed the bedroom door.

Hazel tossed and turned. She was far too excited to sleep. She could envision herself on the back of the beautiful little brown pony, while the pony ran through an open meadow. Hazel with her hands entwined into the pony's thick black mane. In her mind's eye, she saw her red hair whipping out behind her and the pony's tail high and arched flowing behind them.

The next thing she knew it was morning. She heard Sunrise announcing it. He was quite loud and quite persistent.

She jumped up and stood on her bed. She threw open the windows and called, "Good morning Sunrise." He answered her in rooster fashion, "Cock-a-doodle-do."

Two crows swooped down from a tall poplar tree. They circled in the sky high above Sunrise, protesting loudly. They clearly did not like having another feathered newcomer in their neighborhood.

Sunrise cocked his head sideways and studied the sky above him with his left eye. He was determined to hold his post, so he ruffled his feathers and puffed them out, making himself look much larger.

Hazel smiled and thought he was pretty smart. She jumped down from the bed to go get ready for breakfast. She could smell that the sauce for the lasagna had already been started. Her mother liked to simmer it for most of the day. Hazel liked it that way, but today she wished it was already done. Today her mother was going to ask Mary about riding lessons for Hazel. It felt like waiting for

C. S. Crook

Christmas.  She was so excited and it was just so hard to wait.  She got dressed and walked into the kitchen.  Her father was reading the paper over his coffee.

"Well, look who's up," her mother announced cheerfully.

Her father looked up from his paper, "You certainly slept late, Kiddo."

"I woke up just as soon as I heard Sunrise crowing."

"Well, I'll tell you that's one lazy rooster," her mother said.

Her father shook his head in agreement.  "Yep, if my Grandpa had a lazy rooster like that on his farm, he would be having it for dinner the same night."

Hazel looked worried for Sunrise.  "But our neighbors are having lasagna tonight, huh Mommy?"

Her mother shot her father a disapproving look, and then she turned to Hazel and said, "Honey, Sunrise is safe because he is a pet."

 Hazel was visibly relieved as she slid onto her chair at the table.  Her mother placed a plate of scrambled eggs and toast in front of her.  Hazel asked hopefully, "How about I go over and visit our new neighbors while you make the lasagna, Mommy?"

"How about you pick up your room and after lunch we will go over together?"  Her mother gave her a stern look.

Hazel knew that was not really a question at all.  "Yes Mommy," she replied and shoveled the steaming eggs into her mouth.  When she finished her breakfast, she asked to be excused from the table and went in to clean her room.  Between picking up her toys, she would occasionally jump up on her bed and peer out the window to see what was going on next door.  She could just see the rumps of the two ponies and the horse inside their stalls.  She wondered what they were doing.  She wished that they would turn around so that she could have a good look at them.  She looked over at her model horses standing on her shelf.  The real horses were so much bigger and so beautiful.  The morning seemed to drag by.

## The Magic Wishbone

Hazel's mother called to her, "Lunch is ready."

"Finely, I thought lunchtime would never get here!" Hazel said to herself. She sat down to a grilled cheese in front of her and took one bite. "I'm done," she announced.

Her mother was standing in front of the cook stove and looked over her shoulder and said, "Eat more of it."

Hazel let out a big sigh, but obeyed. She really was hungry, but she really wanted to get next door.

Her mother carefully slid the lasagna into a warming bag. "You might want to get ready to go," Jenny said.

Hazel sprang up from her chair, nearly knocking it backwards onto the floor.

"Easy does it, Kiddo," her father said from the doorway. "What's all the excitement about?" he grinned.

"You know, Daddy!"

"I know what?" He pretended innocence.

"I'm starting my riding lessons with Mary. Are you coming?"

"You two go ahead. I've got chores to do."

 Hazel got ready to go in a flash. She and her mother set off for next door. Hazel saw that the two crows were still harassing Sunrise. They were hopping back and forth on the fence line, quite a ways off to his right. They seemed not very sure of themselves. The day was bright and sunny. Hazel saw Jerry in front of the house putting gas in his lawn mower. She and her mother waved to him.

"Good morning," he called out to them.

"Good morning to you, sir," Hazel's mother Jenny replied. "My family and I thought that with the work you folks need to get done we could take a load off for you. We brought you some dinner over."

"That's very nice of you," Jerry said.

"It's lasagna!" Hazel exclaimed.

"That's my favorite! How did you know?" Jerry smiled at her and then at Jenny.

"It is my favorite too!" Hazel said.

"Well isn't that something, we have already have much in common," Jerry told her.

"We do?" Hazel asked.

"Sure we do. We both enjoy lasagna, and horses."

"I sure do," Hazel said. "We have come over to ask Mary about riding lessons."

"Mary will be very happy about that," Jerry said. "Here, let me take that lasagna inside for you. You folks can go on around back; that's where you'll find Mary. She's hardly ever in the house. I think she was born in a barn. I know it's her preferred home."

Jenny handed Jerry the lasagna. "She has time to speak with us?" Jenny asked Jerry.

"Sure, she will enjoy the company, especially the little one."

Jenny and Hazel walked together around the back of the house to the barn. They found Mary in the breezeway of the barn. She had the little brown pony's halter hooked to cross ties while she brushed him. Mary looked up from her work and saw them approaching. "What a nice surprise," Mary said warmly.

"We brought you over some lasagna," Jenny said. "Jerry said that you might have a minute to talk to us."

"I'm never too busy to talk. What's up?"

Hazel could not contain her excitement. Mommy and Daddy say I can take riding lessons, if you say it's alright. Please, please say I can?"

# Chapter 4

"I would be delighted to have you as my very first student here in California."

Hazel's face lit up with joy. "When can I start?"

"You can start right now, if you want too."

Hazel turned and looked at her mother. "Can I, Mommy?"

"If Mary has the time, I see no problem with that."

"Good, then we can get started with Wishbone here."

"Wishbone?" Hazel asked; as she and her mother exchanged looks of surprise.

"Yes, that is his name."

"His name is Wishbone, like as in a magic wishbone?" Hazel asked Mary.

Mary said, "Well yes, see his white marking on his forehead, it is a perfect wishbone. Haven't you ever made a wish buy pulling on a wishbone?"

Jenny was speechless, but Hazel spoke up for both of them, "Yes we have. It was just before you moved into here. What would you like me to do for my first lesson?" Hazel asked, eager to get started.

Mary said, "I was just getting ready to groom Wishbone. I think that would be a good place for us to start. What do you think?"

"I would love to," Hazel replied cheerfully.

Mary bent over a bucket she had sitting near the stall door on the floor of the barn. She stood back up with an oval rubber comb in her left hand and an oblong wooden brush with short stiff bristles in her right hand. "I will show you how to get started. With the rubber curry comb you make circular patterns on his coat. He really likes to be brushed, because it feels like a massage for him. See, look at his face, his eyes are almost closed."

Hazel chuckled. "He looks like a sleepyhead."

"That might have been another really good name for him," Mary said. "Anyway, you just curry one small area and then you brush the area in the direction that the hair grows. But you have to pay attention because it grows in different directions on different parts of the body."

"It does, really?" Hazel asked, surprised.

"Yes, look at the hair here on his flank. See the way his hair kind of fans out in different directions. You need to be careful to brush him softly here, because in the flank area he is ticklish."

"He is?"

"Yes, but not only him, it is true of all horses."

"I'm ticklish to, huh Mommy?"

"Yes, very ticklish," Jenny replied.

Hazel reached out and softly touched Wishbone's smooth coat. "Wow, he is so soft."

"Here, would you like to try?" Mary said holding the brushes out to Hazel.

"I sure would," Hazel said, taking the brushes offered to her.

Jenny studied the contented smile on Hazel's small round face. She looked over at Mary and said, "I'm afraid I may never see her at my house again. We're going to miss her." Hazel looked over at her mother and shot her an ear to ear grin.

"Well, we will enjoy having her," Mary said, smiling and winking at Jenny.

The Magic Wishbone

After a while Hazel worked her way back toward the tail. "How do I brush this?" she asked.

"We don't brush the tail. We pick it with our fingers, because if we combed it or brushed it the hair strands may break."

"Why is that?" Hazel asked.

"The hair in the mane and tail are very course and brittle," Mary replied.

"Oh," Hazel said as she tucked the wooden brush under her left arm and reached out and touched the tail with her little fingers. "It's not at all soft like his coat, how come?"

"His tail is a built-in fly swatter."

"That's funny," Hazel said, as she shot her mother a glance that silently asked, 'is the lady putting me on?'

"No, really, that is what they are for. That, and to also help keep them warm," Mary assured her.

Hazel enjoyed her first lesson. She brushed the entire pony, even underneath his belly. When she was done, Mary took a soft towel and ran it all over his entire body.

"When you brush and curry a horse it brings much of the dirt to the surface. You use the cloth to dust them off. See how his coat shines now?"

"He is just beautiful," Hazel said.

Well, now he is since you did such a good job brushing him," Mary told her.

Hazel beamed proudly. "When can I have another lesson?" she asked.

"We will have a lesson once a week, if your parents agree."

"That will be fine." Jenny said.

"Oh, I can't wait for my next lesson." Hazel announced, while reaching up and running her hand along Wishbone's sleek, long neck.

Jenny said, "We had better let Mary get back to her chores. I'm sure she has a lot to do."

"Thank you, so much, for the lasagna. It's one of Ray's favorites."

"He told us!" Hazel replied.

"Enjoy, and thank you for giving Hazel the lesson," Jenny said

Hazel took her cue from her mother and remembered her manors. "Thank you, Mary; I enjoyed my lesson very much."

"The pleasure has been mine," Mary told them both.

When they returned home Hazel told her mother, "I have to find Daddy and tell him all about my lesson."

Jenny smiled as she watched Hazel run off to find her father. After Hazel told her father all about her first lesson, she got her cardboard sled and took the trek to the grassy hill alone in search for her friends.

Johnny saw Hazel coming toward them in the distance. He left his group of friends and sprinted up the trail toward her, followed by Trouble. "What took you so long? Where have you been?"

Hazel smiled and said, "Johnny, my parents are letting me take horseback riding lessons from Mary and today I had my first lesson. Guess what else?"

"How would I know, what else? But I'm sure you're going to tell me."

"The pony's name is Wishbone!" Hazel squealed and reached out and hugged Johnny tightly.

Hazel's hug surprised Johnny, but he tried not to let on. "Wow, his name is really Wishbone?"

"Yes!  The magic is really working.  Isn't that wonderful!" Hazel said, as they walked toward the group of children at the top of the hill.

Johnny shouted out to their friends, "You guys, Hazel's wish is coming true."

The children gathered around Hazel so that they could hear the latest development. Hazel said, "Mommy and Daddy said that I can take riding lessons from Mary."

"Who's Mary?" Lester asked.

"She is our new neighbor, the riding instructor."

"Oh," was all Lester said.

Hazel continued, "Anyway, I went over there today and had my first lesson with the pony that I wished for and I found out that his name is Wishbone."

"Wow that is neat!" Bobby said, "That must be magic!"

# Chapter 5

Hazel's radiant smile lit up her whole face, "That is what I've been thinking. Nothing else can possibly explain what is happening."

"I would love to take riding lessons," Donna said.

Leslie replied, "Your family is poor, Donna. Poor people don't ride horses."

The children could see tears well up in Donna's eyes and Donna turned and walked up the trail alone toward her home. Hazel glared at Leslie and said, "What makes you so evil, Leslie?" Hazel then ran after Donna. When Hazel caught up to Donna, tears were streaming down Donna's face. Hazel reached out and hugged Donna. Donna wept upon Hazel's shoulder. After a while Hazel said, "Don't you worry, Donna, we will figure something out. Mary is a real nice lady; let me talk her for you. Together we will see what we can do."

Donna pulled back from Hazel's embrace and said, "You would do that for me?"

"Of course, I will do that for you. Now come on, don't let Leslie spoil your fun today." Reluctantly, Donna allowed Hazel to lead her back to the top of the hill.

The very next Saturday morning Jenny took Hazel next door for her second lesson.

"What am I going to learn today?" Hazel asked Mary.

"I think we should pick up where we left off. We will start with the tail and mane. And when we are done with the tail and mane, I will teach you about hoof care."

"Oh, you mean how to care for Wishbone's feet?" Hazel asked.

"Yes, but only we call them hoofs because that is what they are, see how hard they are."

"But, don't they wear shoes? I've heard that horses wear shoes."

"Yes they do wear shoes, but theirs is very different from ours. We will get to that when we get done with the mane and tail." Mary then proceeded to show her how to pick the tail with her fingers. "You take the tail one small section at a time. You hold it in your hand and start at the bottom and work your way up, gently pulling apart the tangled hair."

"It's just like when I comb my hair!" Hazel exclaimed.

"Exactly, that's right. When you are done, we will put it in a tail bag. That will help us to keep it clean and free of tangles. We will not have to do the tail again at your next lesson, if we do that," Mary said smiling at Hazel. "That means less time to work and more time to ride."

"I like that idea," Hazel said.

"I thought you might," Mary replied.

When Hazel completed the task with the pony's tail, Mary showed her how to put on the tail bag. Then they moved on to the mane. When Hazel finished with the mane, she asked Mary, "Is there a mane bag?"

"There is something called a mane tamer that we will use when we get ready to go to a show."

Hazel's eyes widened in surprise at what she had just heard, "I will get to show Wishbone?"

"You will, once you have had enough lessons to prepare you to do so."

"Wow that is something," Jenny said, surprised by the news herself.

"I can't wait to tell Daddy!" Hazel said, grabbing a hold of her mother's arm and bouncing up and down. She could not contain her excitement.

"He will be surprised," Jenny said. "I think it will be a wonderful opportunity for her, Mary. Thank you."

"My goal is to try to get each student to at least one horse show. I don't expect them to win, but rather to just try their best. Learning to be a good sport is just as important as winning."

"Absolutely, I agree," Jenny said.

Mary smiled and replied, "But, before we can do that, we have a long way to go."

"Shall I get started on his feet?" Hazel asked, more eager than ever to get started.

"Hoofs, you mean." Mary said, ruffling her hair gently.

Hazel smiled sheepishly and said, "Hoofs, I meant to say hoofs."

"I always start with the left front hoof," Mary said. "You touch him right here, just above the hoof. It is called the fetlock. You squeeze ever so slightly and presto, he will pick up his hoof for you." As Mary did so, the pony cocked his hoof and rested it on the toe of his hoof. Mary picked up the hoof and held it sole up, facing her. "Look!" She exclaimed. "There is a frog in here."

"Really, where is it? Let me see?" Hazel asked, and both she and her mother stepped closer.

"It's right here," Mary said. The v-shaped pad is called a fog. It provides a cushion to protect the small bones inside the horse's hoof.

"Oh, I thought you meant a real frog," Hazel said.

"I thought Wishbone might have stepped on one," Jenny said.

Mary chuckled, "I just can't help myself. I play that trick on all my new students. But it really is called a frog." Mary reached into the back pocket of her jeans and pulled out a small metal tool with a red handle. It was so small that it fit easily into the palm of her hand. "The tool here in my hand is a hoof pick. You hold the blade away from you and starting at the back of the hoof, you dig all the dirt and manure out from around the frog."

Hazel wrinkled her nose. "Manure, yuk, how come he has manure in his hoofs?"

Both Jenny and Mary glanced at each other and laughed. "He has manure in his hooves because he is a horse," Jenny told her daughter.

"There is a much to learn about life at a stable," Mary told Hazel. "Would you like to give it a try?"

"OK, I guess so," Hazel said. She was a little less enthusiastic than she had been just moments earlier.

"Stand at Wishbone's shoulder, so that you are facing his rear, and rest the front of his hoof in your left hand. See how I'm holding it?" Mary showed her.

Hazel stepped up to Wishbone's shoulder and reached for his hoof with her left hand, just as she was instructed to do. She quickly had to use her other hand also, to keep from dropping the hoof to the ground. "It's so heavy!" She exclaimed.

"They do not help you hold it up at all. We have to do that. Here let me show you a trick." Hazel stepped aside and let Mary take hold of the hoof again.

"Slightly bend your leg, always the leg nearest the horse. Then, you can rest his hoof on your leg while you hold it to clean it. Now you try it." Hazel stepped up and tried again. "Is that better?" Mary said.

Hazel nodded her head in agreement as she vigorously dug to clean out around the frog in Wishbone's hoof.

"You have amazing patience with her," Jenny said to Mary.

Mary shrugged her shoulders and said, "Everyone needs to start at the beginning. The most wonderful thing about a life with horses is you never stop learning. That is what makes a life with horses so intriguing."

"How does the hoof look now?" Hazel asked.

Mary peered down at the hoof and said, "Excellent! Now we have only three more to go!"

"Cleaning hooves is hard work," Hazel said.

"It sure is," Mary agreed with her. "But I would not trade my world for any other. Now we move to the hind leg from here, and then to the front leg on the other side of him."

When Hazel set down Wishbone's front leg he shifted his weight so that he was resting his rear hoof on its toe. She looked at his rear leg apprehensively. "Does he want to kick me?" She asked Mary.

"Oh no, he is just taking his weight off his hoof to make it easier for you to pick up."

"That's nice of him," Hazel said, feeling much more comfortable.

"Yes, he is a pretty nice pony," Mary said, and patted Wishbone affectionately on his shoulder.

Hazel worked her way all the way around the pony. "I'm all done," she said, standing up and stretching her back. "Do I get to learn to ride my next lesson?"

"You will very soon," Mary assured her. "But we must learn the proper care of horses first. We need to know how to take care of our friends."

"What am I going to learn next week?"

"What they eat and drink. You will get to help me feed them."

"I can't wait. That will be so much fun."

"For the next lesson I will need you to be over here a 7:00 am. That is what time they are used to being fed. I hope that is not too early for you folks?"

"No, that will be fine," Jenny said.

After the lesson, Hazel met her friends at the trailhead and they all went to the top of the hill, but Johnny and his other two friends were nowhere in sight. They all left their sleds on top of the grassy slope and set out to find them. They walked in the direction of the Shoreline Lodge. The children had just stepped out from the eucalyptus grove when they spotted Trouble with the three boys at the other end of the meadow. The three boys were all huddled around something that was upon the ground. As the other children approached, they could see that there were three baby raccoons in the tall grass. Fred was the first one to speak, "Where is their mother?"

The forever wise guy James spoke up and said, "You'll have to ask them. Trouble found them here in the grass."

Hazel said, "Well I think we need to leave them alone so their mommy will come back."

Bobby said, "Hazel is right. If the mother coon sees us she will not come near them."

Donna said, "Oh they are so cute, look at them!"

"Yeah, they are cute until they get into your trash can and you have to clean up after them." Fred said.

Bobby said, "Come on you guys, let's leave them be for now. The weather is beautiful today, what do you all say that we go down to the beach?"

Donna said, "I'm all over that idea," and she danced a little jig.

Together, the children entered the woods again and took the trail that veered off into the little valley. The lush ferns underneath the tall pine trees were still wet from the morning fog and glistened in the filtered sunlight. Then the path turned and now the children were following the little stream that ran out to the sea. Along the way, they would occasionally stop to pluck the wild raspberries from the vines that grew up the steep slope to one side of the stream. The raspberries were a deep crimson color and as sweet as they could possibly be. They soon came to the little foot bridge that crossed the stream where the skunk cabbage plants grew so profusely. Robert said, "I will never get used to the smell of skunk cabbage plants."

His big brother said, "Hence the name, skunk cabbage, Robert."

Donna said, "I don't understand how a plant that is that pretty could smell so nasty like that."

Johnny said, "Look at all the bugs on them. The bugs sure seem to like them."

The children were close enough to the ocean now that they could hear the crashing of the waves upon the shoreline echoing throughout the little valley. Seagulls wheeled about in the sky above them searching for their next free meal. The children were starting to get excited as they drew nearer to the beach and Donna skipped ahead of all the others.

The fine silt on the valley floor began to turn into a sandy loam and James stopped to remove his shoes and smiled at the others. "The last one to the water is a rotten egg!"

Fred leveled his gaze at James and said, "OK, James, on the count of three, you're on. Alright, everyone take off your shoes." Fred began the countdown, "One, two, and three!" The children raced toward the incoming waves. They spent the afternoon chasing each other up and down the shoreline, in and out of the waves. They splashed each other and then Johnny come up with a great idea, "Hey, let's have a sandcastle building contest."

Lester said, "What will be the prize for the best castle?"

"I know what the prize can be." James volunteered. The children turned to stare at him. "Leslie has to promise not to pick on you for the rest of the day, if you win."

## The Magic Wishbone

Leslie picked up a handful of sand and said, "I'm getting you for that, James." She sprinted toward him and he took off running down the beach with Leslie in hot pursuit. The other children giggled while watching them.

Robert said, "I think she likes him!"

Bobby said, "I'm glad she likes him and not me." Everyone laughed and then they began to scour the beach for items to embellish their sandcastles with.

Hazel and Donna searched together, "Look Donna, at what I found."

"What is it, Hazel?"

"It is a piece of beautiful dark blue sea glass."

"I would save that and make a necklace out of it."

"How would you do that?" Hazel asked.

"Daddy has special drill bit that he could drill a hole for you to hang a chain. It would look real pretty as a necklace."

Hazel held the dark blue sea glass up and saw the sunlight filter through it. "You think he would really do that for me?"

"Sure, I know he would."

"How about I give the glass to you, and you ask him for me?"

"Of course, I will give it back to you when he is done."

Hazel smiled and handed the sea glass to Donna. "Thank you."

"Don't mention it! It's not a big deal. My daddy likes tinkering with stuff." Together, they found some seashells and small, ornate pieces of driftwood, and even some small crab claws and a crab shell. Hazel was sure that they could trade the claws to the boys for something neat. She knew that boys had an affinity for stuff like that. She and Donna had five crab claws and one crab shell between them. Donna wanted the shell and two of the claws so she and Hazel set out to strike a deal with the boys who had the best pickings. Then each child set out to make a sandcastle that was just as unique as they were individually. Each castle was adorned with what nature had provided upon the coastline. The children didn't worry about who had won the contest as they stood back at the end of that day and watched with satisfaction as the tongues of the high tide licked at the castles until they melted back into the sea from which they had originally come.

On their way back home, the children stopped by the meadow to see if the baby raccoon's mother had returned. She had not. Johnny asked the group, "What do we do now?"

# Chapter 6

Fred said, "If we leave them here, something is going to come along and eat them, for sure."

"They have been here all day without anything to eat or drink," Hazel said. "I know, let's take them to Mary. She likes animals and I'm sure she will know what to do." The children agreed that it was best not to leave them there. Something had happened to the mother raccoon. Hazel reached down to pick up a baby raccoon.

Leslie said, "It's going to bite you!"

Hazel hesitated and James reached down and gently scooped one up into his hands. He held up the baby raccoon for all the other children to see it cradled in his palms.

Johnny said, "Yep, Leslie, it sure does look ferocious." He stooped down and picked up a baby raccoon. Hazel picked up the other one. Together, the children set out for Mary's house.

Jerry heard a gentle rap upon his door. He opened his door and was surprised to see his front stoop crowded with children. He was even more surprised when he saw three of them hold up three baby raccoons in their hands, as if in an offering to him. His eyes swept over all the upturned, hopeful faces and he smiled warmly. "My guess is that all of you are looking for Mary?"

The children all shook their heads in unison. "OK, let's go track her down." Jerry led the way around the back of the house to the horse barn. Mary was just tossing the last flake of hay to the horses when she looked up and saw the group approaching. "My, what a lovely surprise," she said.

Jerry replied, "Mary, you have not seen the least of it yet."

"What is it?" Mary asked, as her curiosity peaked.

Hazel spoke up and said, "Mary, we were all hoping that you could help us." Hazel held up the baby raccoon for Mary to see. "They would have died if we had left them where we found them. Something has happened to their mommy."

Mary reached out and took the baby from out of Hazel's hands and said, "Oh the poor little things."

Mary looked over the children's heads at Jerry. He said, "I know, I will get right on it."

Mary smiled at her husband affectionately and said, "Jerry will build a cage for them. I will go into town and get some kitten milk and tiny bottles for them, but you children need to all make a commitment."

"What kind of commitment?" James asked.

"I will be looking to you to take the babies, when they get just a tiny bit bigger, into the woods and teach them how to forage for food, just like their mother would have. Because when they are able, we are going to release them back into the forest. Now before I take on the project, do I have a commitment from all of you?"

In unison, the children shook their heads in agreement.

Mary said, "Alright, for right now, we can put them in that wooden crate over there by the wall." Mary got the crate and stuffed it with some soft hay. "Alright you children need to scoot along for now, because I need to get to the store and get them some milk. They must be very dehydrated by now. You may come back and see them anytime you like." The children thanked Mary and headed for their homes.

The following evening Hazel was getting ready to go over to Donna's house for a sleepover. "Mommy, is it alright if I invite Donna over next week to our house for a sleepover?"

"I don't see why not," Jenny replied. "Are you almost packed for the night?"

"Almost, I just have to get my horse book. I want to teach Donna about horses," Hazel said.

Jenny smiled at her. "So Mary has turned you into a horse expert now?"

"No, it can't happen right away, Mommy. Mary said it takes a lifetime. But I can share with Donna what I have learned."

"Yes, yes you can. Does Donna like horses?"

Doesn't everyone like horses?" Hazel asked.

"Well, honey, that I don't know."

"OK, I'm all packed up, Mommy."

When Jenny's car pulled into Donna's driveway, Donna and her mother came out of the house to greet Hazel and Jenny.

Donna bounded toward the car with her pig tails flopping about her face like a gangly puppy hound dog. "We get to have pizza tonight," Donna announced gleefully.

"O boy, pizza is my favorite!" Hazel exclaimed. "Do you want me to teach you all about horses?" Hazel asked Donna.

"Oh yes, you know I love horses. Do you love cats and birds too?" Donna asked, as she helped Hazel gather her overnight things from the back of the car.

"I sure do. Did you know that our new neighbors have a rooster?"

Donna's mother, Kelly, smiled at Jenny and said, "It looks like Donna is going to be moving in with you and your family. We don't have any pets."

"Well we don't have many compared to our neighbors," Jenny said, as she followed them up onto the porch. "Hazel, you need to be a little lady and mind Mr. and Mrs. Beck."

"I will Mommy," Hazel said, as she set her overnight case down and reached up with her tan, little arms to give her mother a kiss and hug her goodbye. Jenny bent down to embrace her daughter.

"I'll see you tomorrow. I love you, Mommy. And tell Daddy I love him too."

"I will. I love you too," Jenny said, and walked back to her car. She waved to them before she got inside and drove away.

They stood on the porch and watched her go, waving until she was out of sight.

Kelly said to the girls, "Let's go inside shall we?" Together they turned and entered the house.

"Mommy, can Hazel and I look for frogs in the back yard tonight?"

"Cool," Hazel said, as her eyes brightened.

The two girls looked up at Kelly with bright wide eyes, like puppies begging for table scraps for the first time. The only thing missing were the wagging tails. "You two are tomboys. I was afraid of frogs when I was a little girl."

"But, they're so cute, Mommy, how could you be afraid of them?"

"Frogs and a few other creepy crawly things; all which, I'm certain you two would be tickled to find. You two may go frog hunting, after you put Hazel's things in your room.

The two girls giggled and thanked her and then raced up the stairs to Donna's room. It was the room of an animal lover. Posters of kittens, puppies, hamsters and, yes, even reptiles filled the walls. A large stuffed snake coiled around a bed post at the foot of Donna's bed. Ceramic frogs with marble eyes peeked over the edge of a shelf; they seemed to be peering down at the two girls. It was the room of an animal lover, that was for sure, but it was the room of an animal lover who had no animals of her own to love.

The two girls dropped Hazel's belongings on top of the bed and raced back down the stairs to the back door.

"No frogs in the house young ladies," Donna's mother called out to them, as they streaked past her.

"OK, Mom," Donna replied. "I'll show you where the frogs like to hang out," Donna told Hazel. "My teacher calls it their habitat. My whole back yard is their habitat. We'll see if there are any pollywogs in our pond yet."

"Can we catch the pollywogs?" Hazel asked.

"Yep, I've got a jar. I keep it right out here by the pond, just in case," Donna said,

"It's catch and release. That's Daddy's rules," Donna added. "Daddy likes frogs and Mom is warming up to them a tiny bit, because they eat bugs. She really doesn't like bugs."

"She wouldn't make it over where we live," Hazel said.

"Nah, I'm afraid she would not," Donna agreed. "She wouldn't like living that close to the woods, she's a city girl."

"But you guys live here in the country."

"Only because Daddy took her away from the city. She agreed very reluctantly is what she says."

Donna and Hazel approached the pond and kneeled beside it and peered into the shallow clear water.

"Wow, look the pollywogs are so big!" Hazel exclaimed, bending down for a closer examination, until she was on all fours.

"Aren't they something? Donna asked with pride.

"I'll say they are," Hazel said, clearly impressed. "You have a great habitat."

"Wait until you see the frogs. They aren't big like you would think they would be with pollywogs that size, but they have huge voices. You would think they were toads."

"How can we find them?" Hazel asked.

"The best way is as soon as the sun goes down. We wait for them to start croaking and we flush them out with our flashlights, as simple as that!" Donna smiled with certainty.

The girls scooped some of the pollywogs up into Donna's jar and watched them swim about for a bit and then released them back into the pond. They had just started to look for the frogs, although it was a bit too early for real frog hunting when Donna's mother called out from the kitchen window, "The pizza is here."

They ceased all hunting activity and headed for the back door. "I'm starved," Donna announced to her mother, as soon as the two girls entered the kitchen.

Kelly said warmly, "How about you, Hazel, are you hungry?"

"Yes, I'm practically starved too," Hazel assured her.

"Well, my goodness, it looks like the food got here just in the nick of time!" Donna's mother exclaimed, and hurried to get the girls their drinks.

As the two girls chatted and enjoyed their pizza and soft drinks, the sun sank on the horizon bringing forth the dusk. It was nearly perfect frog hunting time. The two girls finished their meal and placed their dishes in the sink and then headed up to Donna's room. There, Hazel took out her book and asked Donna, "Would you like me to teach you about horses?" Donna nodded her head in eager agreement. Hazel turned the pages of the picture book slowly, pausing so Donna would have time to appreciate the true beauty and magnificence of the horses.

"The color of the horse on this page is a Bay," Hazel told Donna. "It says here that a bay horse is brown, with black legs, mane and tail, just like Wishbone. I wish I would have had a chance last night to show you the rest of Mary's horses, but it was so late by the time we took the raccoons over there and Mary had to hurry to the store to get their food," Hazel said, and turned the page. "The red horse here is called a sorrel. It says here that they usually have red manes and tails, but can sometimes have flaxen manes and tails."

"What does flaxen mean?" Donna asked

"It beats me. Hey, I've got an idea!" Hazel said, "The next time you see Mary, you can ask her. She is a horse expert."

Donna smiled, "I can't wait to see her horses and rooster too." Donna looked toward the window, "Listen did you hear that?"

Hazel looked up from her book, "Hear what?" Hazel asked.

# Chapter 7

A frog croaked loud and clear, "Did you hear it that time?" Donna asked, grinning from ear to ear. "It's time to go frog hunting." Donna jumped up from where she had been sitting and grabbed her flash light off her dresser. "Let's go get them!" Donna exclaimed, with excitement ringing clear in her voice.

Hazel closed her book and laid it on the bed beside her and sprang up to follow Donna down the stairs.

"We're going hunting, Mom," Donna called out to her mother, as the two girls headed for the back door.

"I do not want one frog in the house!" Her mother shook a warning finger at them from the doorway of the den.

"I know it, Mommy," Donna replied.

Donna stepped out onto the back porch and held the screen door open for Hazel. As soon as Hazel stepped through the doorway, Donna very softly closed the door. She held a finger up to her mouth and whispered, "Shush, we have to be very quiet so we can sneak up on them."

Hazel followed Donna, who held her flashlight poised ready for the action of the hunt. A moment of silence fell over the yard. Donna stopped in her tracks and Hazel nearly bumped into her in the dark yard. Donna put one out stretched arm down to her side, her fingers extended; Donna was motioning for Hazel to be still. Donna slowly lifted her flash light. Then, just as the frogs begin to converse anew with each other, Donna flooded the pond with light and moved with the speed of a sun-soaked reptile. She pounced and with one fell scoop of her fingers, she had the poor unsuspecting amphibian clenched in her hand. Donna had plucked it from the bank of the pond. "Hazel, could you get me a pollywog jar?" Donna asked softly.

"They are right over there." Donna pitched her beam of light across the little pond, illuminating where the small glass jars rested.

Hazel picked up a wide mouth jar and unscrewed the lid and held it out to Donna. Donna slipped her tiny hand into the jar and let the frog slide gently from her hand until it rested on the bottom of the jar. "Now quick, put the lid on, just the second that I remove my hand. They sure can jump."

Hazel followed the instructions and secured the top of the lid. The yard had fallen into silence at the first beam of the flashlight. "Let's go into the garage, and check him out. And later, we can come back out here and hunt some more. They know we're here. We have to wait until they forget about us."

They went into the garage and Donna turned on the overhead lights. Then she proudly held up the jar to show Hazel their prize. "But he is so tiny!" Hazel exclaimed. "Is it a baby frog?"

"Nope, he is as big as they get," Donna said

"But I thought they would be huge because of the loud noise that they make," Hazel said.

"I know. Sometimes, they are so loud it disrupts my sleep. It sounds like they are having a frog party almost every warm night."

"We have many crickets where I live. The crickets are pretty noisy at night too," Hazel said, and took the jar from Donna and slowly turned it. The little frog sat huddled on the bottom of the jar. "I think he is afraid."

"Yeah, probably so, I think he is afraid we're going to eat him."

"He is really cute. I feel bad that he is afraid," Hazel said.

Donna said. "Listen, I can hear the frogs again. We have time to catch one more. But remember to be very quiet, because they are quick."

"What do you want me to do with him? Do you want me to bring him?" Hazel asked.

"You can just set him there on top of Daddy's work bench for now. We have more jars by the pond," Donna said.

"He won't be afraid by himself?" Hazel asked.

"Nope, I don't think so. We will be right back with one of his buddies," Donna assured her.

The two girls went single file again back out into the yard towards the pond. Hazel was tiptoeing across the lawn. She was less self-assured in the dark yard then Donna was. When they reached the ponds bank, Donna was poised with her flashlight held high, ready to pounce once more when the yard was suddenly awash with light.

"Girls, it is time to come in now" Donna's mother called to them from the back porch.

"Oh, mom, I almost had another one!" Donna whined.

Kelly told her firmly, "You'll just have to catch it another night. It's late. Little girls should not be out in the dark late at night."

"OK, OK, but we have one in the garage that we have to set free," Donna told her mother.

"I'm sure you do. As soon as you let it loose, you girls come in for the night."

"Yes, ma'am," Hazel said politely.

On their way back into the garage, Donna told Hazel, "I hate it when that happens. You almost have a frog and then the hunt is blown at the last second."

"I know that's just parents," Hazel agreed with her.

Donna picked up the jar off the work bench and said to the frog. "Come on, little buddy, it's your bed time too. Let's turn him loose, but here just outside the door so we can watch him hop away." Donna replied and unscrewed the jar and gently slid the frog out onto the ground. Eagerly, the frog leapt away and the flashlight beam followed him until he disappeared into the plants that

46

surrounded the little pond. Donna turned to Hazel and said, "I love frogs. I wish I could keep some in my room. I could make a little habitat out of a fish tank. Like, you know, how they have in the pet stores. I know I could make him happy. I would be so nice to him."

Hazel shook her head in agreement. "I know any pet would be lucky to have you as an owner."

"Mommy says that I can have all the pets I want when I grow up and get my own place." Donna sighed and added, "That is such a long time. And Daddy says that the frogs are much happier out here by the pond then they would be in a terrarium in my room."

"Maybe when you grow up you can be a vet, so you can be around animals all day long. That's what I want to be," Hazel said.

"I want to be a veterinarian too! I can't think of anything that I would love to be more than a veterinarian," Donna said.

Donna and Hazel went into the house and got ready for bed. After they were both in bed, Donna's mother came in and kissed Donna goodnight. "Sleep well you two, and keep it down to a dull roar."

The two girls giggled as they lay side by side in Donna's bed.

"Good night, Mrs. Beck."

The following morning, Hazel woke before Donna. The sunlight was streaming into the bedroom, illuminating the selves that lined Donna's walls. The creatures stood on the selves like sentries guarding a kingdom. They were plastic and glass creatures from all over the world. They looked like they would be more suited for a boy's room, but they could not be more loved than where they stood guard.

Hazel could hear Donna's mother down in the kitchen. The aroma of coffee floated up the stairs. Hazel gently shook Donna's shoulder. "Donna, wake up sleepy head."

Donna yawned and stretched and opened her eyes slowly to the brilliant morning. She startled when she realized that there was someone else with her in her bed. "Okay, now I'm wide awake," she said, trying in vain to mask her initial alarm.

Hazel laughed, "Donna, you were afraid!"

"That's it. I owe you one," Donna retorted.

"Hey, it's not my fault that you didn't remember that I was here."

"Well, you enjoyed that a little too much, I owe you one."

"Girls breakfast is on," Kelly called up the stairs.

Kelly had made a handsome stack of French toast and sausage to go with it.

"Yum, breakfast looks delicious, Mrs. Beck."

"I thought you might like French toast," Kelly said

"I sure do, especially with sausage.  It just goes together like pancakes and bacon."

Kelly smiled and said, "Yes, I suppose you are right."

After the two girls had breakfast, Donna and her mother gave Hazel a ride home.  The two girls agreed to meet up that afternoon at the trailhead.  Hazel was not in her own home long before she asked her mother, "Is it alright if I go over to see if Mary needs any help with the baby raccoons?"

"I think that is a marvelous idea, Hazel, so poor Mary will not think that you children just dropped all the baby raccoons in her lap and forgot about them.  But do not stay so long that you are a pest."

Hazel smiled and said, "I would never do such a thing." Then she dashed out the door.  Hazel found Mary and Jerry out at the barn. Jerry was busy building a cage for the baby raccoons and Mary was sitting on a bale of hay feeding one with the other two in her lap when Hazel walked into the barn.

"Good morning, Hazel," Jerry said, as he looked up from his work.

The Magic Wishbone

"Good morning, Mr. and Mrs. Adolf, I just came over to see if I can give the two of you a hand with the baby raccoons?"

Mary smiled at Hazel and said, "Your timing could not have been more perfect. I was just starting to feed them. Would you like to do it?"

A wide grin spread across Hazel's face and she said, "I would love to feed them."

"That would be wonderful, because I always have other choirs to do. Please come over anytime you or the other children like to feed them when you can. I will give you their feeding schedule and if any of you can't make it, I will wait for fifteen minutes before I will go ahead and feed them."

Hazel sat down on the bale of hay next to Mary and replied, "I know all of my friends would love to help feed them."

"Well, perhaps all of you could get together and figure out a schedule amongst yourselves."

"Sure, I will be happy to talk to them about that today. I'm sure everyone would love the idea of taking turns to care for the little cuties."

"They would have certainly perished if it had not been for the kindness of you and your friends."

"We can't forget the kindness of you and Jerry and you're willingness to help us foster the babies."

Mary said, "We are all animal lovers, the whole group of us. We shall get along quite fabulously! Well you go ahead and feed them and I will go clean stalls."

Hazel nodded and took the baby raccoon and the tiny doll bottle from Mary and put the bottle to the raccoon's lips. To Hazel's surprise and delight, the baby raccoon latched onto the nipple of the bottle and sucked vigorously. Hazel giggled and Jerry smiled at her and just shook his head. He knew that not only did he have his Mary that was an insatiable animal lover, but now he had a whole group of them. He knew that he could not have asked for a better life. Each of the baby critters took to the bottle with the same enthusiasm and Hazel let them each drink their fill. Jerry had just finished stapling the last of the wire onto the cage where they were going to be temporally housed. Hazel helped him fill it with soft hay for their bedding and Jerry attached a bottle of water to the side of the cage. He said to Hazel, "This is usually used to water rabbits. A bowl of water would be more ideal, but I'm afraid they are a bit too young for that just yet. I'm afraid they would spill it, and they don't have their momma to keep them warm."

Hazel nodded and said, "I've heard that they love to wash their food in water before they eat it."

"Exactly, that is why a bowl of water for them would be more ideal. Raccoons are very resourceful. It should not be very hard for us to reintegrate them back into the wild."

"I want to thank you, Jerry, for building them the cage."

"Don't mention it, kid, I'm happy to do it, now we let's see how they like it."

Hazel brought the crate over to the cage and she very gently placed one baby raccoon at a time down upon the billowing pile of hay. When all three of the raccoons were snuggled together, she smiled and looked up at Jerry with satisfaction upon her face. He grinned back at her and snapped a locking clasp on the cage door. "The lock is going to have to be replaced with something more suitable in the very near future. They are very clever critters. They can break into and out of just about anything that you can throw at them."

Just then, Mary walked up and handed Hazel a slip of paper, "I've written down their feeding schedule, so that you can share that with your friends."

"Thank you, Mary. I don't want to make a pest of myself, so I will see you guys later."

The Magic Wishbone

Mary smiled warmly and said, "Hazel, you could never be a pest. We will look forward to seeing you." Hazel left and returned home for lunch and then she set out for the trailhead to meet up with her friends. When they all met up with Johnny, James and Robert on the top of the grassy hill, they all set their sleds aside and sat down in a large round circle and discussed the feeding schedule of the baby raccoons. Since Hazel lived right next door to Mary, they all agreed that she would take the first and last feeding of the day. Johnny would take the feeding just before the noon hour and so forth. Donna was so excited that she begged everyone to let her take the very next feeding which was within the next hour. They all played on the slope with their sleds until it was time for Donna to leave to feed the babies. Johnny and Hazel decided to tag along with her. As they walked along on the trail back toward Hazel's house, Hazel said to the other two children, "While we are there, I will show the two of you Wishbone. I think he is so beautiful."

"I want to see that rooster! I have never seen a friendly rooster." Johnny said.

# Chapter 8

Hazel replied, "His name is Sunrise and he sure is friendly. Mary just seems to have a way with animals, according to what her husband says."

Donna was all starry-eyed as she said, "I just can't wait to hold the baby raccoons and feed them."

Hazel said, "It was so much fun feeding the raccoons. They were such hungry little things."

"Can I feed the babies first and then we can look at the horses?"

Hazel smiled and said, "Sure thing, Donna, that will be fine by me." Donna smiled and gave herself a little hug because she was just so excited.

When they reached Mary's house, Mary showed them how to mix up the milk formula and Donna sat down on a bale of hay to feed the first baby. Donna's two companions sat on each side of her and looked on. Donna giggled and said, "Look at the milk flowing down both sides of its little mouth, how precious is this?"

"It sure is a cute little thing," Johnny said. Trouble sat next to Johnny and watched intently, with both of his large ears forward and alert as the little varmint guzzled its milk. Johnny reached out and gave Trouble a good ear scratch, "Because of you the little raccoons are alive." Trouble wagged his tail vigorously, as if he understood what Johnny had said to him. Donna rocked the baby raccoons in her arms as she fed each one. When Donna was finished feeding the raccoons and they were safely placed back upon their nest of hay, Hazel said, "Oh I almost forgot." She reached into the pocket of her jeans and took out the piece of blue sea glass, which now had a long silver chain attached to it. "Turn around Donna and hold up your hair so I can put the necklace on you."

Donna did as she was instructed but said as she did so, "Why are you putting your necklace on me?"

After Hazel closed the clasp she gently turned Donna around and said, "Here let me see how it looks on you?" Hazel smiled and shot a sideways glance at Johnny and asked him, "What do think, Johnny, doesn't the blue match her eyes?"

"Yeah, I suppose so."

Donna reached up and touched the sea glass pendant and asked again, "Why are you putting your necklace on me?"

"Because my friend, it was never intended for me. It was yours all along."

"Oh, Hazel, thank you, the necklace is beautiful. I had no idea that you were planning to give it to me."

"Duh, that is why they are called surprises. Besides, it matches your baby blue eyes."

Johnny spoke up and said, "It would of clashed with Hazel's green eyes anyway, Donna."

"It is just so nice of you, Hazel. I have never had anyone do something so nice for me."

Hazel replied, "That is what friends are for, to make you feel special once in a while. Now let's go see the horses."

Donna beamed brightly and said, "I want to see Wishbone first."

Hazel led the way to Wishbone's stall and stopped in front of his stall door and whistled softly. Wishbone had his back turned to them and stretched his long slender neck around to look at the three children standing on the other side of the double-Dutch doors.

Donna audibly sucked her breath in and said, "Hazel, he is beautiful. Look, he does have the markings of a Wishbone on his forehead!"

Hazel said, "I told you he did, that's why Mary named him Wishbone. That is why it is magic, I wished for a pony using a wishbone and here he is just days later." Wishbone nickered softly to the children and turned around and put his head over the stall door to greet them. Hazel reached out and softly ran her hand along his face to his soft muzzle. She felt his warm breath on the palm of her hand. "Go ahead, you can pet him. He is very friendly."

Johnny reached a hesitant hand out to touch the pony's sleek neck and Trouble stepped protectively between Johnny and the stall door. Wishbone lowered his head and sniffed at the dog. Trouble lifted his head and sniffed the pony's nose and then licked it. Donna said, "Look, Trouble just kissed Wishbone!" All three of the children laughed with joy at the unique interaction between the pony and the dog. Trouble looked up at Johnny and waged his tail.

Johnny said, "I think Trouble is trying to tell me that the pony is A-OK!" Johnny then ran his hand down the full length of the pony's neck. "His coat feels like silk, Hazel!"

"Mary takes such good care of her horses. She cares for them from the inside out!"

"What does that mean?" Donna asked.

"I'm only beginning to learn that myself, Donna, but I will teach you that as I learn all about it in my lessons." Donna ran her slender fingers through the pony's sleek mane with a dreamy look on her face.

"Come on," Hazel said, "I'll show you the other horses."

The next stall belonged to Sunny the sorrel horse. "This big and beautiful guy is Sunny," Hazel said. "He is Mary's personal riding horse, but she said that she uses him in lessons also for her more advanced riders."

"Wow," Johnny said, "That horse has a lightning bolt mark on its face."

"That is called a blaze," Hazel said.

## The Magic Wishbone

The buckskin pony stuck its head over its stall door and looked quizzically at the children and the dog. Hazel continued her tour of the barn for her friends, "The buckskin here is Dakota. Mary said she starts all her students out on either Wishbone or Dakota. Dakota is also very gentle, but also a little stubborn and will take advantage of you, if she gets a chance. Mary said that Dakota is too wise for her own good sometimes."

"Dakota is very pretty!" Johnny said.

"Mary say's that pretty is as pretty does. She also says that you can't judge a horse by its color, "Hazel said.

"Oh, there is so much to learn about horses!" Donna said.

"Mary told me that it takes a lifetime to learn about them and even with all of that there is still more to know. She said that is why they are so interesting and fun!" Hazel said, with a huge grin.

"Dakota has kind of a lightning bolt on her face too. Why do you want Wishbone? I think Dakota is much prettier, Hazel?" Johnny said.

"Wishbone is the magic pony. I know he is the one that is meant for me. Like I said, I don't understand how magic works, but all I know is that it is working."

Donna smiled and said, "Johnny, pretty is, as pretty does!"

Johnny rolled his eyes at Donna and said, "Whatever that means, Donna! You were going to show me the friendly rooster, Hazel, where is he?"

Hazel smiled at her two friends and led the way out of the barn and into the sunlit barnyard. "He is usually hanging out here somewhere this time of the day. They rounded the corner of the barn and found Sunrise scratching for grubs underneath a large pine tree. The three children saw a car pull into the circular driveway of Mary's yard. Mary came out onto her porch to greet her new guest. The three children saw Leslie and her mother step out of the car. Leslie spied the other children and sprinted toward them. She ran up to them and said smugly, "Mommy is here to get me started on riding lessons so I can learn all about horses, because I want to buy Wishbone! Mommy says that I need to learn how to care for him first."

Hazel's two other friends turned to look at Hazel just in time to see the color leave Hazel's face and tears beginning to well up in her eyes.

"Leslie!" Leslie's mother called out to her.

Leslie smiled brightly at Hazel's reaction and said, "Well, I need to go take care of business!"

Blinded by her tears Hazel turned and stumbled in the direction of her own house, flanked on either side by her two friends. Hazel's mother was in the yard hanging laundry on the clothesline. Hazel ran sobbing broken heartily toward her mother. Hazel's mother dropped her dress that she had been about ready to pin back into the basket and stretched her arms out toward her daughter. Hazel ran into her mother's waiting arms and buried her face into her mother's bosom.

"What on earth happened?" Jenny asked. Hazel was sobbing so hard that her shoulders were shaking and she could not speak.

Donna spoke up and said, "Mean old Leslie has asked her parents to buy Wishbone for her, because she knows that Hazel wished for him before he showed up here."

"Is that what they are doing now, they are buying him right now?" Jenny asked alarmed.

Johnny spoke up and said, "No, Leslie said that her mother wants Leslie to learn how to take care of him first. They are there to inquire about riding lessons."

Jenny looked visibly relieved. "We will see you later, Hazel," Johnny said, Then, he turned to Donna and said, "Come on, Donna, let's go." Johnny was surprised when Hazel turned away from her mother and reached out and gave Johnny a tight hug and then she hugged Donna. "Thank you both for being my friends," she said weakly, with a trembling smile upon her lips. Donna and Johnny walked away glancing back several times as they went, while Jenny led her daughter by the hand and sat down with her upon the steps of their front porch. "So Leslie only wants Wishbone because she knows that you wished for him?"

Hazel wiped at her eyes and shook her head in affirmation and said, "She has never even seen him before, Mommy."

# Chapter 9

"But there are two ponies over there, surly she could choose the other one?"

"I hope so, Mommy. Johnny even said that he thinks Dakota is prettier than Wishbone is. But you just don't know Leslie; I think she likes to be mean on purpose."

Jenny placed her arm over Hazel's shoulder and said, "Oh I don't think anyone is mean on purpose, sometimes they just don't know how to act is all."

"Well then, she doesn't know how to act much of the time, Mommy. She even told Donna that Donna can't take riding lessons because poor people don't ride horses."

"That just is not true," Jenny said. "There are many of poor people who ride horses all over the world. Donna's family is not poor. That was an unkind thing for Leslie to say. Leslie has no idea what being poor really is."

"I'm going to talk to Mary to see if there is some way that Donna can take lessons. I know that she is a very nice lady, she will figure something out," Hazel said.

Jenny wrapped both of her arms around Hazel and planted a kiss on top of her head and said, "You are a true friend, Hazel. I'm proud to be your mother."

The next morning Hazel did exactly that. When she got done feeding the baby raccoons, she approached Mary when Mary was mucking out a stall. "Mary, my friend Donna's parents don't have very much money and she would really love to take lessons from you. She loves animals of all kinds, but doesn't have any. Is there some way that we can figure out a way that she can take lessons?"

# The Magic Wishbone

Mary put both of her gloved hands upon the top of the handle of the pitchfork that she had been using and rested her chin upon them and studied Hazel for a moment before she replied. "Is that the same Donna that came over here with you to feed the babies' yesterday morning?"

Hazel nodded and said, "Yes, that is her."

"You don't think her parents would mind, if she worked over here?"

Hazel was feeling hopeful for Donna now and smiled broadly and said, "I don't think they would mind at all."

"Well you ask your friend, Donna, to bring one of her parents over here and we will work something out.

"Oh, Mary, you are the best!" Hazel said and hugged her. And then Hazel asked Mary, "Is Leslie going to buy Wishbone?"

Mary saw the clear look of concern on Hazel's little face. "No," Mary replied.

"But Leslie told me that her parents are getting her riding lessons so she can learn how to take care of him."

"They would like to buy him. They did ask me about the possibility of purchasing him, but he is not for sale."

Hazel's face became radiant and she bounced around Mary with sheer joy. Mary smiled at her and said, "I thought you would be pleased. Leslie told me something yesterday that I wanted to ask you about?"

"Sure, what is it?" Hazel said.

"Leslie told me that you made a wish on Thanksgiving Day with a magic Wishbone and that you wished for a pony. She said that you thought that your wish had come true. Is that true? Did that really happen?"

Hazel cast her eyes down at the ground and said, "I didn't mean that I wanted to take your pony." Then she looked up into Mary's eyes and said, "I just don't know how magic works."

"Then it is true."

Hazel looked fearful and Mary quickly said, "Hazel, you're not in any kind of trouble. I just think that is an amazing story. Why didn't you tell me about that?"

"My mommy didn't think it would be proper to say anything about it, because Wishbone belongs to you."

"Well, Leslie is going to be taking lessons with us and I'm sure that in time I can find another suitable mount for her when her parents are ready to make a purchase."

"I want to thank you, Mary, for not selling Wishbone. And thank you for letting Donna take riding lessons."

"We will have to wait and see what Donna's parents have to say."

Hazel nodded and replied, "I will give Donna the message this afternoon. I will see you later, Mary."

"All right, Hazel, you have fun with your friends today." Mary watched the little red headed girl with the freckled face walk away and was reminded of her own horse-crazy youth.

After lunch, Hazel met her friends at the trailhead with their sleds and they all went to meet Johnny and their other friends. On the walk to the top of the hill, Leslie boasted to Hazel, "Well, it looks like your magic is not working, Hazel."

"Why do you say that, Leslie?" Hazel asked.

Fred jumped into the conversation, and said, "When did you become the authority on magic, Leslie?"

Leslie ignored Fred's comment and replied to Hazel, "I say that because Wishbone is not for sale, so therefore he will never be your horse."

Bobby said, "Never is a long time, Leslie."

Lester spoke up and asked, "Leslie is there ever a morning that you get up and say to yourself, 'I'm not going to be mean to anyone all day.'?

"I'm telling on you, Lester!"

"You are telling on me for speaking the truth, Leslie?"

"I'm telling on you for making fun of me!"

"You always seem to manage that all on your own, Leslie," Fred said.

"Humph!" Leslie said, and stomped up ahead of the others.

Hazel waited until they reached the top of the hill and pulled Donna aside out of earshot of the others. "Donna, Mary said that if you are willing to help her with choirs around the barn, she will give you riding lessons, if your parents agree to it." Donna let out a squeal of delight and grabbed Hazel and squeezed her tightly. The other children turned their heads and looked at Hazel and Donna, but had no idea what that was up. "Mary wants you to go over to her house with one of your parents to have a discussion about it."

"Thank you, Hazel, you have no idea how much it means to me!"

Hazel smiled and said, "We will get to see each other more often. Come on, let's go ride our sleds."

The two girls walked back over and joined the rest of the group and Leslie asked, "What was all that squealing about?"

Donna looked Leslie straight in the eye and while smiling smugly said, "Nothing, Leslie."

"You just go ahead and suit yourself, Donna."

"I'm just following your lead, Leslie."

"What is that supposed to mean, Donna?"

"I'm sure you can go figure it out for yourself. You seem to know so much today," Donna said. Leslie glared at Donna and then Leslie set her sled on the ground at the lip of the hilltop and prepared to launch off.

Johnny walked up and got in line behind Hazel, "Hey, Hazel."

"Hey, Johnny, how are you?"

"I'm good. How did the baby coons eat for you this morning?"

Hazel shot him one of her beautiful smiles and said, "Like gluttons."

He grinned back at her and said, "Yeah, me too!"

Donna interjected, "They are getting so big already."

"They sure are," Johnny agreed, and then added, "Mary told me that soon we will be able to take them out into the woods to teach them how to eat grubs and stuff."

Fred walked up just in time to hear the last statement, and said, "Yummy!"

Donna looked up at Fred and wrinkled her nose and said, "You're gross, Fred!"

Hazel sighed and said, "He is just a normal boy, Donna."

"That makes me glad, I'm a girl," Donna replied. Hazel smiled at her in an unspoken agreement.

James walked up on the tail end of the conversation and said, "For me that is going to be the fun part, taking them into the woods and teaching them how to fend for themselves."

"I like to feed them with the bottle!" Donna said with a bright smile.

James replied, "That's because you are a girl." Donna nodded in happy agreement. When the children were done playing on the hill for the day, Johnny said to James and Robert, "I'm going over to

Mary's with Hazel and Donna to watch Donna feed the baby coons, do you guys want to come?"

Robert and James both shook their heads no and Robert said, "You go ahead and go with your two girlfriends, we'll see you at dinner at the lodge."

Johnny picked up a dirt clod and chucked it playfully at Robert. Robert ducked and chuckled as he walked away with his older brother. Johnny snuck a look in Hazel's direction and she had the rosy glow of a blush on her cheeks. Johnny and Trouble walked with the large group of children until Johnny split off from the larger group with the two girls. They walked along in comfortable silence until they reached Mary's little ranchette. Johnny walked over to the little refrigerator in the barn and took out a bottle of milk that was already mixed and shook it vigorously and he handed it to Donna, "Here, I mixed the formula up for you after I fed them before lunch."

"Thank you, Johnny," Donna said, as she took the bottle from him. Donna then peeked into the cage and said, "Which one of you gets to be fed first?" The baby raccoons came chattering up to the door and one climbed up the wire of the door. Donna stuck her tiny little figure through the wire mesh and gently rubbed its belly. "It looks like there is a clear winner!" Donna said happily, as she unclipped the lock on the door and swung it open with the baby raccoon still hanging on, but only with one front and hind leg. Donna smiled and gently pried it free and closed the cage. She cuddled the baby raccoon to her chest as she walked over to the hay bale and sat down to feed it. Johnny and Hazel sat down on either side of her. Donna offered the raccoon the nipple of the bottle and the baby latched on to it and ripped at it with its newly emerging baby teeth.

Johnny chuckled at the sight and said, "I'm sure glad that wasn't my finger!"

Hazel laughed and said, "Me too, Johnny."

Donna looked down at the little critter cradled in her arms and said, "Do you hear the little slurping sounds? How cute is that?"

"Way too cute!" Hazel said in agreement.

C. S. Crook

Johnny said, "Its tummy is going to pop, Donna, if you don't stop feeding it and give another one a turn."

Donna held the baby raccoon up and looked at its tummy and smiled. "Yep, just about ready to pop. Back you go," she said. Then, she stood up and returned it to the cage and got another one. "I think I might need some more milk, Johnny, after I fed this one."

"I know that you are going to need some more milk," Johnny said. Trouble laid at Johnny's feet and watched intently as the little raccoons had their meal. Sunrise strutted in from the sunlit barnyard and Trouble sat up with both of his large ears pointed straight at the large rooster. Johnny instantly tensed up at the sight of the rooster. Sunrise paid them no mind and went about his business of looking for tasty insects. Johnny relaxed and said, "I still just can't get used to seeing a friendly rooster. If that had been the one we had back home in Texas, it would already have us by now."

Hazel said, "Well then, I'm glad Sunrise isn't like the rooster that you used to have."

"We had a nice big pot of chicken and dumplings made out of him, just before we left the desert."

Donna looked at Johnny horrified and said, "You ate your pet?"

Johnny replied, "Oh, he was no pet! That you can rest assured of. It was his job to keep the hens laying eggs."

"Well, why did you eat him?" Donna wanted to know.

64

# Chapter 10

"He went and got himself killed. It wasn't me that did it, and anyway it was an accident. There was no use in letting good chicken meat go to waste. But I must say he sure did taste good all stewed up in dumplings."

"Johnny, would you please mix me up some more of the milk? The bottle is almost empty."

Johnny got up off the bale of hay and said, "Sure, Donna, I will make it right now." After Donna fed the last baby, the children all dispersed to their respective homes for the evening.

The next morning was time for Hazel's third riding lesson and she was so excited. She found Mary in the barn, "Good morning, Mary."

"Good morning, Hazel," she said and handed Hazel Wishbone's halter. Hazel took the halter and studied it for a moment. Mary smiled at Hazel and said, "It can tricky at first putting the halter on."

"There are so many openings, it's hard to see where his nose goes," Hazel replied.

Mary reached for the halter and took it from Hazel's hands, "Here let me show you a trick. See the buckle? It always goes on the left side of the horses head just below its left ear. So, if you hold it up with the halter already buckled you can see where his nose goes." Mary smiled and handed the halter back to Hazel. Hazel took the halter, feeling more confident. She stepped into Wishbone's stall and slipped the halter over his soft muzzle and buckled the halter into place. Mary smiled and handed Hazel the lead rope. Hazel snapped it into place just underneath Wishbone's muzzle and led him from the stall.

"Oh, that is something that we need to work on first thing," Mary said.

C. S. Crook

"What do we need work on?"

"The proper way to lead a horse is the safe way. In my lessons, I teach safety first. Wishbone is a wonderful pony, but even he can be startled, just as you and I. Here, let me show you something." Mary took the lead rope from Hazel's hand and Hazel stepped back and watched Mary. Mary said, "See, I've placed my body here, just at the front of his left shoulder, but I have my arm outstretched, putting my body an arm's length away from him. So if he shied from something and tried to bolt, I would be out of harm's way, because he is very big. Then, I could just let him run in a circle around me. The other thing is, I see experienced horse people, even some with more experience than I have, loosely coil the lead rope around their hand. That is a very dangerous practice because, if your horse gets spooked and bolts, that rope within seconds can become like a knot from the tension and trap your hand inside. People have lost fingers doing that or worse; some have even been dragged to their deaths." Hazel's eyes opened wide at the last statement. Mary saw her reaction and said, "I'm not telling you the information to frighten you and make you afraid of horses. I'm teaching you how to stay safe, because someday you may go on to ride very large horses that are way more spirited than Wishbone. The information will keep you safe for your whole life around horses. So, instead of coiling the rope around your fingers, fold it like an accordion and hold it inside your hand and the rope can feed out if need be." Mary smiled and handed Hazel the lead rope and said, "Here, you try it now." Hazel stepped up next to Wishbone and followed Mary's instructions. "That is a very good job, Hazel." Mary said, beaming proudly at Hazel.

"Now we can move on to tacking up. Go ahead and take him over there in the breezeway of the barn and hook him up to the cross ties." Hazel led Wishbone over and hooked him up to the cross ties. Mary said, "I always start my students off in a Western saddle and later, as they advance, I teach them how to ride in an English saddle." Mary showed Hazel how to put on the saddle and talked about why the saddle was placed exactly where it was and why on the horses body.

"Wow, there is just so much to learn!" Hazel said.

# The Magic Wishbone

Mary smiled and replied, "That is what makes horses so much fun. It can take an entire lifetime to learn everything. It never gets boring or stale. We have covered a lot today and the great news is, your next lesson is going to be in the saddle."

A wide smile spread across Hazel's face, "I can't wait, Mary!"

"You are a very quick learner, Hazel. It has been a real pleasure teaching you so far."

After Hazel returned Wishbone to his stall, she saw Fred and Johnny followed by Trouble coming into the barnyard. "Hi, guys, have you come to feed the baby raccoons?"

"Yep, it is Fred's turn," Johnny replied. Hazel walked into the barn with her two friends. One baby raccoons climbed up onto the wire siding of the cage and started chattering quite loudly.

"That is Chatter," Fred said. "He does that every time he sees me."

Hazel looked at Fred in amazement and asked, "How can you tell them apart?"

"Because he is the only one that does that," Fred said.

"I've thought before that we should name them, but I can't tell which one is which," Johnny said.

Fred went over to the refrigerator, and took out the bottle that someone had already mixed up for him. He opened the cage and gently pried Chatter's little claws from the wire. "OK, you little glutton, as usual you get to be fed first." All three of the children took their places upon the bale of hay and enjoyed watching the hungry little varmint eagerly attack the nipple on the bottle. "Look at the way he is chewing up the nipple. Let's ask Mary if she thinks we should start taking them into the woods yet. I think they are ready to start learning how to survive on their own."

Johnny shook his head in agreement, "I think you are right, Fred. It looks like time by the way they all attack that bottle." As the children were just finishing up feeding the babies, Mary walked into the barn followed by Sunrise. Johnny looked up at the two odd

67

companions and said to Mary, "That rooster follows you around just like a dog or something."

Mary chuckled and said, "He does have an identity problem, that is for sure."

Fred asked Mary, "Do you think it would be alright if we took the coons into the woods today to see if they are ready to start learning how to fend for themselves?"

"I think that is a marvelous idea!" Mary replied.

Fred was quick to form a plan, "OK, we will all come and pick them up just after lunch. We will spend all afternoon helping them find food and letting them play in the woods for a bit."

Mary looked at the three adorable children sitting on the bale of hay and said, "Splendid, I know that they are going to enjoy their outing. They have such inquisitive little minds. I'm sure they are growing bored being trapped inside that cage."

After feeding the last raccoon and returning it to its cage, Fred said, "Alright then, Mary, we will come back over right after lunch and get them."

"That will be good. I will see the three of you then." The children all said their farewells' to Mary and headed for their homes.

After their lunch the children returned to Mary's barn. The children were very excited to see how the baby raccoons would fare on their very first outing since they had been orphaned. Johnny said, "I think we should take them to the huckleberry bushes."

Bobby said, "I was thinking of starting them out looking for grubs."

"Yuck," Leslie said, "That is disgusting."

"Just be glad you're not a raccoon then, Leslie," Fred said. Then he went on to add, "I think for their first meal on solid food the grubs would be good for them, because grubs are full of protein for them."

"I think so, too!" Hazel said.

Johnny looked at Hazel and then at his two other friends and said, "OK, then grubs it will be." The six boys let the three girls carry the raccoons into the woods.

On the way Leslie asked, "Where are we going to find grubs?"

"That is a silly question, Leslie," Robert said.

"What do you mean that is a silly question, Robert?" Donna demanded to know. "I was just wondering the same thing myself."

Robert lifted his arms up and spun around in a circle as he said, "They are everywhere." The other five boys all nodded in agreement.

James said, "You just have to know where to look for them is all."

"Oh that must be what my problem is then, I'm not used to looking for maggots," Leslie said.

Donna wrinkled up her nose and said, "Gross, Leslie, did you really have to say that?"

"Well, that is what they are, Donna," Leslie said.

"They are not maggots, Leslie. That is why they are called grubs," Robert said.

Leslie retorted, "Maggots and grubs are the same thing!"

Robert vehemently disagreed, "They are not!"

"They are!" Leslie stood her ground.

Robert demanded to know, "Then why are they bigger, sometimes?"

Leslie retorted, "Because they are bigger maggots, silly."

Fred interjected, "Forget it, Robert. Dad says that you can never win an argument with a woman and I'm starting to understand his point." Leslie gave Robert a triumphal smile. Robert just shook his head in disgust and let the debate drop. They walked along a little bit farther and Fred said, "Look at all of the old, decaying, tree limbs right here. It looks like just as good of a spot as any." The other boys nodded their heads in agreement. Fred reached down, and turned a rotten tree limb over. It broke apart easily, even crumbling in some places.

Donna peered at the decayed chunks of wood, "I don't see anything."

Bobby said, "There is only one way to find out for sure."

"What is that, Bobby?" Hazel asked.

"We will put the coons down right in the center of it. If there are grubs in there they will find them." The three girls placed all the raccoons in the center of the richly brown colored decayed wood. The little raccoons went to work right away, much to the surprise and delight of all the children. The raccoons put their noses to the pile of debris beneath of their tiny little paws and like scent tracking dogs, they meticulously worked through the rotten wood, often turning pieces over for a closer inspection. One raccoon looked up at the group of children and excitedly made a chattering noise.

Fred said, "Look, Chatter, has already found something." And sure enough, Chatter picked a plump grub up with his tiny hands and stuffed it into his mouth and chewed with delight.

"That is gross! I can't stand to watch that!" Leslie said.

"That is as cute as can be!" Lester said. "The little guy is having his first real meal."

Fred added gleefully, "It is a historical moment, Leslie, and you are going to miss it! Oh boy, yummy, maggots are for dinner!" All the boys laughed.

Leslie said as she lunged for Fred, "I'm getting you, Fred, for that!"

Soon, the baby raccoons became more interested in playing than they were in eating. They scampered about upon the decayed tree limbs and chased each other. Chatter stopped his play momentarily to look up at Fred, and another baby raccoon pounced upon Chatter from behind, bowling him over. The children laughed at the comical sight. After a long while of roughhousing, the three babies lay panting upon their fat bellies. Johnny said, "I think they are going to sleep really well tonight."

"They tired me out just watching them," James said.

"I can just see the three of them all grown up and in someone's trash can," said Fred.

"Yep," Bobby said, "they would leave a mess all the way from here to Mendocino."

Fred walked over, and picked up one of the raccoons and said, "Come on, Chatter, it looks like your bedtime."

"How do you know that is Chatter?" Leslie demand to know.

Fred looked at her and asked, "Leslie, have you ever owned a pet?"

"No."

Fred replied, "I thought that would be the answer."

"That still doesn't answer my question!"

Johnny walked over and picked up one of the other babies and as he walked passed her he said, "Figure it out, Leslie." James scooped up the last raccoon and all the rest of the children fell into line and headed back to Mary's house.

# Chapter 11

The next day after lunch, when Hazel set out to join her friends at the trailhead, she saw Johnny emerge from Mary's driveway. "What a surprise, Johnny. Didn't you get to have lunch yet?" Hazel asked.

"Yes, I was just letting Mary know that all of us would like to take the raccoons out into the woods again today."

Hazel replied, "That was sure a lot of fun yesterday, if not more than a little bit gross."

"I'm hoping that we will grow used to seeing them eating the grubs," said Johnny.

"I hope that you are right."

When the two children reached the trailhead, Leslie promptly announced, "Daddy said anything is for sale, if you offer enough money for it. Daddy said that I'm getting Wishbone for my Christmas gift!"

Hazel couldn't believe what she had just heard. She wanted to pinch herself, to wake herself up from the horrible nightmare. Donna looked at her best friend and saw the blood drain from Hazel's face, but it was Johnny who caught Hazel, just as her knees buckled and she went reeling toward the ground. Johnny gently lowered Hazel to the ground and placed her head in his lap. Johnny looked up at Donna and said, "Run, go get her mother." Donna looked hesitant to leave her friend, but then sprang into action and sprinted away. Johnny glared up at Leslie and said, "I hope you are happy with yourself, now."

Leslie looked uneasily around herself and down at Hazel upon the ground, "I had no idea that was going to happen." She looked in the distance and saw Jenny and Mary running toward them. Donna was trailing behind, nearly out of breath. Leslie panicked and ran for her home. She wanted no trouble with the grown-ups. She knew her mother would protect her.

Hazel's eyes flickered open and she looked up into Johnny's concerned face. It was funny that she had never noticed before how beautiful his blue eyes were. "What happened," she asked in confusion.

Just then Jenny rushed up kneeled beside her daughter. Mary leaned down and placed a cool hand upon Hazel's brow. "She is awfully warm to the touch, Jenny."

Panting, Donna stepped up to the small circle that had gathered around Hazel and said, "She fainted because Leslie said that her father is going to buy Wishbone for Leslie for a Christmas gift."

"I thought that matter had already been settled," Jenny said and looked at Mary.

"This is the first that I have heard about this," Mary said.

Hazel's eyes filled with tears and they streamed down her flushed cheeks, "Please, Mary, don't sell him?"

Mary looked at the feverish little girl that lay upon the ground. Hazel's pleading tear-filled eyes just melted Mary's heart. "I'm not going to sell Wishbone to Leslie, Hazel; you can rest assured of that."

"Mary, could you please help me get her back home?" Jenny asked. Together the two adults helped Hazel to her feet and with one adult on each side they slowly walked Hazel home and put her to bed.

At the trailhead Lester said, "I'm sorry for how poorly Leslie has been acting lately."

Johnny looked at him and said, "Lester, it's not your fault." Then Johnny turned to the group and said, "Come on, let's go get the raccoons and introduce them to huckleberries today." The remaining children followed; Donna was the only girl among all the boys. They let her carry one of the raccoons and Fred got to carry Chatter to the nearest huckleberry patch.

Johnny, along with the other children, watched the antics of the babies as they climb in the huckleberry bushes. The raccoons loved the huckleberries. Soon their little mouths were stained a dark purple-blue from the berries. Often the raccoons would fall from the bush, only to climb clumsily back up and sink their teeth back into one of the sweet little orbs that dangled from a branch. Johnny enjoyed watching the babies, but he worried about Hazel and wished that she could be here to enjoy the moment with her friends.

Hazel swiftly recovered from her flu and soon joined her other friends in the raccoon adventures in the woods. One day Hazel said, "The raccoons are growing so quickly that we should get started looking for a suitable home in the woods for them."

Robert said, "Hey, how about that old shed down in the valley by the beach?"

James said, "There are many different kinds of berries down there."

Leslie said, "If they live in the shed something could come in and get them."

Robert said, "They will live underneath it. Raccoons are smart; they live underneath old buildings all the time."

"Oh, I'm going to miss them," Donna said.

"I have no doubt that we are going to be seeing much more of them then we want to," said Fred.

Johnny looked at Fred and grinned, "In the trash cans?"

"Yep," Fred replied.

The next time the children saw Mary, they asked her what she thought about their plan. Mary said, "I think that is a marvelous idea! Christmas is nearly here and what would be a better gift for our little friends than freedom?" Smiles lit up on the children's faces.

A week before Christmas the children took the raccoons into the woods and started to introduce them to their water source that was

The Magic Wishbone

near the shed.  They used huckleberries and made a little trail from the shed to the water source.  The children started the raccoons at the shed and watched as they munched their way to the little stream.  And then the boys lined the trail back again to the shed with grubs.  The raccoons loved the stream and spent quite a bit of time playing with the pebbles in the water.  Then, on Christmas Eve, Mary gave the children a flake of hay for bedding for the raccoons and the children poked the hay as far under the old shed that they could reach. And with tears in his eyes, Fred kissed the top of Chatter's head and placed him upon the nest of hay.  Donna, with tears running down her round little cheeks, hugged one of the other raccoons to her chest one last time and handed it to Fred.  Fred gently, placed it next to its sibling.  Hazel kissed the last raccoon and said "Keep yourself safe!"  She then handed it off to Fred.  The children who were not openly crying were doing so inside.  They all loved the little raccoons that fate had temporarily entrusted into their care.

On Christmas morning, Hazel walked into the living room.  The Christmas tree was all lit up and the smell of fresh pine needles filled the air.  "Merry Christmas, Hazel," Jenny said cheerfully from behind her.  Hazel turned to see her mother, smiling behind her.

Hazel said, "Merry Christmas, Mommy.  Where is Daddy?"

"He is out in the front yard.  He has something that he would like to show you. Put on your shoes and a coat, it's chilly out."

Hazel did as she was asked and walked to the front door with her mother.  Just as her mother was pulling open the door, Jenny said, "Hazel, wishes do come true!"

Hazel looked up at her mother baffled and when the door opened, it revealed her father standing out on the front lawn with Wishbone.  Wishbone had a huge Christmas wreath around his neck and a Santa Claus hat between his ears.  Hazel jumped from the front porch and ran across the lawn and threw her arms around Wishbones neck. She never wanted to let go!

C. S. Crook

Please write a review on Amazon.com. It will be greatly appreciated.

The Magic Wishbone

Also in this series are the books, 'Johnny's Reptile Adventure,' book 1, 'The Skipper's Captain,' book 2, 'Johnny's Heroic Adventure,' book 3, and 'Finding a Home,' book 4.

**Johnny's Reptile Adventure** (Johnny's Adventure Book 1)
**by C.S. Crook**
**Link:** http://amzn.com/B00LDCEPQY


**The Skipper's Captain** (Johnny's Adventure Book 2)
**by C.S. Crook**
**Link:** http://amzn.com/B00LR89PSW


**Johnny's Heroic Adventure** (Johnny's Adventure Book 3)
**by C.S. Crook**
**Link:** http://amzn.com/B00MD7O2Y8


**Finding a Home** (Johnny's Adventure Book 4)
**by C.S. Crook**
**Link:** http://amzn.com/B00MDYI7EC


**The Magic Wishbone** (Johnny's Adventure Book 5)
**by C.S. Crook**
**Link:** http://amzn.com/1503278832


**Johnny's Treasure Adventure** (Johnny's Adventure Book 6)
**by C.S. Crook**
**Link:** http://amzn.com/B0159IY7AQ

Made in the USA
Middletown, DE
29 October 2016